D1456995

ALPHABEARS

An ABC Book

By Kathleen Hague

Illustrated by Michael Hague

Henry Holt and Company
NEW YORK

Henry Holt and Company, LLC
Publishers since 1866
175 Fifth Avenue
New York, New York 10010
www.HenryHoltKids.com

Library of Congress Cataloging-in-Publication Data
Hague, Kathleen.
Alphabears: an ABC book.
Summary: Introduces a bear for each letter of the
alphabet and describes its special qualities in rhyme.
[1. Alphabet. 2. Bears—Fiction. 3. Stories in
rhyme.] I. Hague, Michael, ill. II. Title.
PZ8.3.H1193 1984 [E] 83-26476

ISBN 978-0-8050-1637-6
15 17 19 20 18 16

First published in hardcover in 1984
by Henry Holt and Company
First paperback edition—1991
Printed in February 2010 in Mexico by R. R. Donnelley & Sons Company,
Reynosa, Tamaulipas

To Devon, who's just like his Pop. —K.H.
To my old teddy bear, Potts. —M.H.

A is for Amanda, a good teddy bear
Who carries sweet apples everywhere.

B is for Byron, who snuggles in bed
Mom tucks him in with a kiss on the head.

C is for Charles, a stuffy old bear

He wears a bow tie and a part in his hair.

D is for Devon, who's just like his pop

Their noses are big and their ears sort of

flop.

n exploring bear

jungle because it was there.

F is for Freddie, a big frightful mess

What he has been up to no one can guess.

G is for Gilbert, a gruff grizzly bear

Whenever he growls you'd better beware.

H is for Henry, who loves his hot cakes
With honey and butter like his mom makes.

I is for Ivan, an itchy brown bear

He loves to be scratched—first here, then there.

J is for John, who loves jam and jelly

It's easy to see, just look at his belly.

K is for Kyle, a kite-flying bear

He loves days that are breezy and fair.

L is for Laura, who doesn't like lightning
She thinks that the sound of thunder is frightening.

M is for Marc, a mysterious bear

Whenever you visit, you won't find him there.

N is for Nikki—that's just her nickname

Her real name is Ninny, her mother's to blame.

O is for Ollie, a one-year-old bear

He's just learned to walk, but can't climb a stair.

P is for Pam, who loves a parade

She also likes popcorn and pink lemonade.

Q is for Quimbly, a soft quilted bear

Who was sewn by hand with much love and care.

R is for Robert, who thinks that it's great
To sit by the fire and read until late.

S is for Sarah, a snow-loving bear

Just give her a hat and warm mittens to wear.

T is for Tammy, who wrinkles her nose

When you tickle her tummy, her chin, or her toes.

U is for Ursula, a quite useless bear

Who seems to do nothing but just sit and stare.

V is for Vera, a kind gentle vet

She lovingly takes care of anyone's pet.

W is for William, the great wonder bear

He wears a white cape and soars through the air.

X is the way that this bear marks his place
So when he returns he can find the same space.

Y is for York, who's a very young bear

To sit at the table he needs a high chair.

Z is for Zak, who says that it is true

That zippers do better than buttons can do.

From Amanda to Zak, the bears are at ease

Because now they can say their A, B, Cs.